Dear Parent:
Your child's love of rea

Every child learns to read in a different way and at his or her own speed. Some go back and forth between reading levels and read favorite books again and again. Others read through each level in order. You can help your young reader improve and become more confident by encouraging his or her own interests and abilities. From books your child reads with you to the first books he or she reads alone, there are I Can Read Books for every stage of reading:

SHARED READING
Basic language, word repetition, and whimsical illustrations, ideal for sharing with your emergent reader

BEGINNING READING
Short sentences, familiar words, and simple concepts for children eager to read on their own

READING WITH HELP
Engaging stories, longer sentences, and language play for developing readers

READING ALONE
Complex plots, challenging vocabulary, and high-interest topics for the independent reader

I Can Read Books have introduced children to the joy of reading since 1957. Featuring award-winning authors and illustrators and a fabulous cast of beloved characters, I Can Read Books set the standard for beginning readers.

A lifetime of discovery begins with the magical words **"I Can Read!"**

Visit www.icanread.com for information
on enriching your child's reading experience.

Balzer + Bray is an imprint of HarperCollins Publishers.
I Can Read® and I Can Read Book® are trademarks of HarperCollins Publishers.
Fox versus Fox
Copyright © 2024 by Corey R. Tabor
All rights reserved. Manufactured in Malaysia.
No part of this book may be used or reproduced in any manner whatsoever without written permission except
in the case of brief quotations embodied in critical articles and reviews. For information address HarperCollins
Children's Books, a division of HarperCollins Publishers, 195 Broadway, New York, NY 10007.
www.icanread.com

Library of Congress Control Number: 2023937523
ISBN 978-0-06-327793-9 (trade bdg.) — ISBN 978-0-06-327795-3 (pbk.)

The artist used pencil, colored pencil, and watercolor, assembled digitally, to create the illustrations for this
book.
Typography by Dana Fritts
Title hand lettering by Alexandra Snowdon
24 25 26 27 28   COS   10 9 8 7 6 5 4 3 2 1 First Edition

SHARED
**My
First**
READING

I Can Read!

FOX
versus
FOX

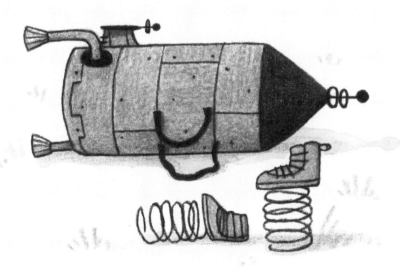

Corey R. Tabor

BALZER + BRAY

An Imprint of HarperCollins*Publishers*

Hi, I am Fox!

No, I am Fox.

I am Fox, too!

Hmm.

Foxes can do tricks.

I can do tricks!

flip

Foxes are sneaky.

I am sneaky!

Foxes can jump.

I can jump!

Foxes can jump higher.

I can jump higher!

But foxes cannot fly.

puff
puff

No, foxes cannot fly.

Foxes are brave, though.

Yes, foxes are very brave.

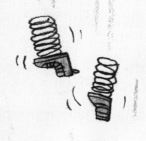

Can foxes swim?

We will find out!

Glub glub glub.

Glub glub glub!

Hmm.

Foxes are friends.

Yes, foxes are friends.